Sleighed By Love

CORAL COVE

BOOK ONE

JAX WILDER

Sleighed By Love

A Steamy, Coral Cove, Santa Love Romance

Sleighed By Love© 2023 by Jax Wilder
Rainbow Quartz Publishing

RAINBOW QUARTZ PUBLISHING

COVER ART BY RAINBOW QUARTZ PUBLISHING

IG: RAINBOW QUARTZ PUBLISHING

HTTPS://RQPUBLISHING.COM/

ISBN: 978-1-961714-02-1

❀ Created with Vellum

Dedication

For the women who enjoy Christmas as much as I do. This story is for you.

Jax Wilder

Santa Baby plays over the radio for the umpteenth time, and I think to myself, if I hear this song one more time, I might start throwing books.

At the same time, a customer walks by and says, "I love this song so much." She has a big grin and a stack of books in her hands. I breathe out my petty annoyance and put on my best customer service face.

"Did you find everything okay?" I ask.

"I found more than enough," she smiles, still humming along to the song. "Your shop is so cute. I love the décor so much. Great costume, by the way. It's got such a fun vibe. I feel like I could spend hours in here."

"Some folks do," I say. I ring up her books and note a tall, dark-haired man from a distance.

My breath catches.

The woman grabs another book off the counter and adds it to the stack, pulling my attention back.

I don't have time for distractions.

"Are you visiting for the tree lighting ceremony?" I ask as I ring up her last book.

When I glance back, he's gone.

"We are. My kiddos are making a last-minute Christmas list for Santa at the toy store. I left my husband with them while I snuck out here. You know how it is," she waves me away as if to imply some universal truth about books and husbands.

"Oh sure," I offer and hand her a receipt. "I hope you enjoy the events. Definitely check out the other little shops around town. We appreciate the business more than you'll ever know."

"I will!" She leaves with her bag and a smile.

Another woman approaches with two books in hand. "I want to get a gift for my best friend. He's gay and loves romance. Which of these two do you recommend?"

I point to the first book, "This one will leave him with smiles from beginning to end." I point to the second, "This one will fill his heart with joy, then it will rip it out, stomp on it, and leave him shredded forever, wondering why." I give her my best toothy grin. "I recommend both of them. One to tear him down and one to build him up."

"Done. I'll take them."

The next forty minutes go by in a blur like this. One customer after another. Coral Cove is a primarily sleepy town. I save my pennies during tourist season and town events because they get me through the seasonal downslides when two customers in a day doesn't pay the rent.

My back is to the counter when I hear another book placed on it. I spin around and come face to face with the tall, dark-haired man from earlier. Somehow, I'd forgotten he was still here.

"Did you find everything okay?" I ask.

"I'm not sure what I'm looking for yet. I did find a couple of books, though," he holds up a copy of *Sleighed By*

Love, written by Lea Steele, and a copy of *From A Youth A Fountain Did Flow* by Miranda Levi.

Right about now, my face is turning twenty shades of red. "These are an interesting pair. Is it a gift?" I ask, ringing up his purchases.

"Maybe? I'm not sure yet. Just trying to do my part to support local," he says.

Does that mean he knows it's my book? Or did he just like the cover? I mean, Levi's book is good, too. Maybe he's just supporting female authors? "We appreciate your business," I say.

"Look, I'm new to town. My name is Alex."

He pauses expectantly.

"I'm Lea," I say. "Nice to meet you, Alex."

Alex tilts his head. "How long have you been working here?"

I sigh, doing the math in my head. "I guess it's been nearly ten or eleven years. I was just out of high school when I started here. I only bought the place myself four years ago. I worked for the older woman who owned it before me. She's passed on now."

"I'm sorry for your loss."

I don't know what to say. "It's okay, she was a bit of a grump. I got to make this place my own. Really embrace my inner geeky girl."

"I like it. I was here once before, and I really enjoy what you've done with the atmosphere. You capture something special in this place. It's like both coming home and finding magic for the first time. Remarkable."

Now, it's me who's taken aback. "Thank you." I itch at the fake ears I'm wearing today and smile. "It's not common to have a full-on themed place around these parts. I just wanted something special. A little different, you know?"

"I think you nailed it. The décor is all anyone in town

can talk about," he says. "Not that I'm eavesdropping or anything, just hard not to hear sometimes."

I shake my head as if I can shake away his compliment. "Can I get you anything else?"

"How about your phone number?" Alex smiles.

"Excuse me?"

"Was that too forward?"

He looks so earnest. Honest even.

"Okay," I say. "I can't promise anything, but I might have some time later, around four."

"Four sounds perfect." His smile makes my legs go weak.

"It was lovely meeting you, Lea. I'll text you and hope to see you at four."

Another customer approaches before I could hear the bell on the door indicating Alex had left the building. I'm off whooshing around the corner to help him find the books on his daughter's Christmas wish list.

When I get around to checking my phone, I find a text from an unknown number.

Unknown Number: Hey Lea, it's Alex. If you're still up for it, how about we meet at the tree lighting? 4pm.

"What's got you smiling?" Park, my one and only employee asks.

"Nothing."

"Liar."

I roll my eyes. "It's just a message from someone asking me to meet them at the tree lighting."

"Who are we dating?" Park snuggles up close to peek at my phone.

"I'm not dating anyone. It was just a customer from today. He was being flirty and asked for my number," I shrug. "I don't know."

"You gave it to him? Oh, girl!"

"What?" I elbow Park. "You're always saying how I need to put myself out there more."

"Good for you."

"I didn't say I was going."

"Yes, you are. What's his name?" Park asks.

"Alex."

Park reaches for my ears, removing the silicone elf ears I wore to match my green and red holiday dress. "There. Now put your jacket on and get your butt out there."

"Are you sure you've got this?" I ask.

"Yeah, no worries. You go enjoy the lights, boss," Park grabs a pile of books that need reshelving.

"Could you also reshelve the stack in children's? Those moms really went to town."

Park chuckles, "I got you. Now go. You're way behind on cuffing season already."

"As if I'm going to meet Mr. Right at the tree lighting."

"Maybe you just focus on meeting Mr. Right Now, instead?" Park winks.

"Goodbye," I say, leaving Park to watch the store.

TWO

Coming to Coral Cove was random. I closed my eyes and tossed a dart at a map. It could have landed anywhere. When I walked into Spellbound Stories, I was looking for an overnight distraction. That's precisely what I found in the form of a curvy redhead. I walked through the doors, transported into a bookstore disguised as a fantasy magic shop. Every inch of this place has been thoughtfully crafted with care.

As a bibliophile passionate about folklore, stepping into Spellbound Stories was a treat. A Tree of Life bookcase that also serves as a staircase in the middle of the main floor leads to the second. Every piece of furniture, art, and product placement has been carefully crafted to create an illusion of fantasy.

If there's one thing I understand better than anything else, it's fantasy, dreams, and desire.

I beeline for a rack of books titled *Noteworthy Folklore Retellings*, where I snag a book about the personification of the fountain of youth. I continue to navigate this art installation disguised as a bookstore.

A woman wearing a floor-length red and green dress, hugging her exquisitely thick thighs, bends over to grab a book. When she stands up, I notice she's wearing elf ears to match the holiday-themed fairy dress.

I suck in an audible breath. I've never been so turned on. "Who is she?" I say, but of course, I already know.

"That's Lea," says a guy with black hair wearing a cape.

"I'm sorry, I didn't realize I'd spoken out loud," I say, taking measure of this stranger.

He waves me away. "She's a goddess. It happens to me, too, and I'm gay."

I chuckle, but I can't deny it. She is a goddess. I nod my agreement.

"She's my best friend," he says, then looks down at his outfit, "and boss."

I raise an eyebrow. "Are you her matchmaker too?"

"Only around the holidays."

This makes me smile. "I'm Alex."

"Park."

"Nice to meet you, Park," I cross my arms. I'm not sure how far I want this conversation to go. It's one thing to know about Lea in my own way. It's another for a guy to feed me information.

"Lea is a writer and entrepreneur. She doesn't get out much because she's always here or writing."

"Why me?" I ask with genuine curiosity. "You don't know me from Adam."

"There's a twinkle in your eye. Something about your vibe is honest and good. I have a feeling about you. Plus, I saw the way you looked at her. I have a sixth sense about these things, Alex."

"And if you're wrong?" I ask incredulously.

Park raises an eyebrow. "Am I?"

"Not even a little," I confess.

Park hands me a book. "You didn't get it from me."

I turn it over, *Sleighed By Love*, written by Lea Steele. "Thanks?"

"Don't thank me yet. If she finds out I'm the one who pointed her book out, she'll kill us both."

"Noted," I add her novel to my pile.

"Don't prove me wrong, Alex," Park straightens a couple of books and walks away to help a guy find a copy of Colleen Hoover's newest book as a holiday gift for his wife.

Coral Cove is quiet, picturesque, and surrounded by water. A guy could get used to it. I text Lea and await her reply in a little bakery while inhaling three of the most delicious sugar cookies I've ever had.

And I've had more than my share of cookies.

My phone beeps and my heart thumps so loud I'm sure the couple sitting at the table beside me can hear it.

It's Lea.

> Lea: Sure, I'd love to meet up. I'll be the one in the Santa hat.

She has no idea what her words do to me.

I type my reply quickly, telling her I'm looking forward to it, and I check the clock. I have ten minutes, which happens to be the perfect amount of time to grab more sugar cookies. I'm guessing Lea would love one of these. Never arrive empty-handed to a date. I think I read that once.

When I arrive at the tree lighting, I can't help but laugh out loud. There are two hundred people gathered, and they're all wearing Santa hats.

Lea's funny. I like that.

Her fiery hair isn't hard to spot in the crowd. "Cookie?" I hold the bag open to her. "They are the most mouthwatering sugar cookies I've ever had. I'm a cookie dude. Ten out of ten would recommend."

"I'll let Dottie know you say so. She's one of the best bakers I've ever known." Lea sticks her hand in the bag and pulls out a Santa hat. "Cute."

"Just sticking to the apparent theme," I smile and am taken by her eyes. I grab another cookie as the tree-lighting ceremony begins.

THREE

Lea

"Thanks for grabbing us peppermint hot cocoa," I say, holding mine with both hands and letting the warmth steam my lips. "I've never been much for the holidays, but I love the lights and this community. Oh, and these," I raise my cup.

Alex tilts his head, sipping his cocoa. "Not too big on the holidays?"

I shrug. "I guess I just think they should be about something more than presents." I put up a hand, "I say this knowing full well that I keep my little bookstore running largely on things like the holidays."

"I can understand that," Alex points down a row of lit houses. "Should we walk?"

"Yes, I love the lights." We stroll down a street lit with bright red and green Christmas lights.

"Holidays should be about more than gifts. What about your family?" Alex asks.

"Not much to tell, really. Mom died years ago, and my dad isn't part of my life. I don't really have anyone else. This town is my family. But they don't warm a bed on a cold night," my cheeks flush. I take a long drag of my cocoa. "What about you? Is anyone warming your bed at night? Family to celebrate the holidays with?"

Alex points to a Santa on a brightly lit lawn. "I love that," he chuckles a low rumble. "I am as single as they come. I have a full-time job in the family business. I'm relatively close to my parents. And in fact, I'm taking over as the head honcho in the business. I did a trial run last year, and this is my first year on my own. My dad wants me to settle down and settle in first. But I think I'm ready. Plus, he and my mom deserve a break. They give so much. This feels like the one thing I can give them."

"I don't want to overstep, but do you want to go into the family business?" I ask.

Alex nods thoughtfully. "I've had a lot of time to think about this. I've grown up with this image of myself taking over one day. It was always a given." He sips his cocoa. "When I was in my late teens and early twenties, I was determined to do anything but. I traveled and went away to school. I've seen the whole of this glorious world, Lea, and my favorite place is home."

I point to a house with one of those projectors in the window. Santa is laughing with a jolly belly and little elves tossing presents.

Alex shakes his head. "So many assumptions," he chuckles.

"Where's home?" I ask.

"North," he says.

"Why so cryptic?"

"Sorry," Alex stumbles over his thoughts with his hands. As if he's not sure what to say. "Not being cryptic at all, we just say the north back home." He smiles. "I live north, as in Canada. Northern Canada, where it snows all the time. It looks a lot like this, actually. There are just not as many folks around. Much colder."

I can't help the smile that plays on my lips. I want to smile just because he's around me. But alas, I also knew it was too good to be true. He's from another country. He's not made long for this one. I pointedly didn't ask how long he'd been here for. There are only a few more days until Christmas. I can only imagine it's short. I'm not going to disappoint myself before it starts.

"What about you? Where are you from? Or have you always lived in Coral Cove?" Alex bumps my shoulder playfully as we continue our walk.

"Teenage rebellion and youthful ambition. I saved up all my after-school money. It was, go to college or get away from the crappy town and the even smaller life I was leading. Simply put, I needed to get away for the sake of my own life." I take a deep breath, not wanting to lay all of it on a man I've just met. But also feeling like, somehow, I could. "I didn't have the best childhood. One day, I applied for jobs all over the state. This was the first place I was offered one. So I took it and moved. Turns out, it was the best decision I ever made."

"This place suits you," Alex says.

I roll my eyes, "Sure, sure. I bet you say that to all the women you meet on your random holiday vacations." This time, I bump his shoulder playfully.

"For real though, I mean what I said," Alex winks.

"Thank you. I appreciate that. This town is my family. I am who I am today because the community gave me a place to stretch my wings," I expand my arms, tossing my empty cup into a trash can.

"And she's so smooth too."

"Darn right, I am." I lead Alex around the corner and to

the back of my apartment. "Do you want to come up? I was thinking of ordering some takeout for dinner."

Alex hesitates.

"No pressure, man. I was just enjoying this, but it's okay." I turn my back on him to unlock the door. My face scorches with embarrassment.

So dumb. What was I thinking?

"Lea, I would very much like to come up and continue our conversation. I just don't want to overstay my welcome or accept if you're only inviting me out of a feeling of obligation."

I turn to face Alex and take in the honesty of his eyes. The softness of his mouth. The desire building in my belly.

I hold the door open for him, and he follows me up.

Alex takes measure of my tiny apartment while taking his jacket off. "It's four days till Christmas, and you don't have a single decoration? I'm confused. I assumed you at least enjoyed the holidays."

I shrug. "I love the town events, like the tree lighting and Christmas lights. But what's the point of putting up a tree? I don't own any decorations. It's still going to be without presents on Christmas morning. Instead of opening the bookstore, I'll sleep in and watch a movie. I usually order extra takeout on Christmas Eve, so I don't have to cook on Christmas Day. That's about as good as it gets."

"So, you really don't spend it with your family?" Alex's eyes are soft. Soulful.

I shake my head, "Nope. It was a mental health and safety choice. Be alone and safe, but alone. Or spend time with my dysfunctional family and be strung out for the next several months on the old and new trauma mingled into my brain and body. Maybe it's selfish, but I pick me."

"No, it's not selfish. I'm proud of you. A lot of people can't do what you're doing. Too much guilt. You just keep doing whatever feels right for you. I'm never going to judge you." Alex is settled on my couch.

This tall, gruff man, with a beard for days, makes my couch look minuscule.

It's not.

I order us some dinner, and Alex insists on paying for it. I let him, mostly because I haven't had someone buy me dinner in ages.

It's nice.

It's kind of sweet, even.

"What do you write?" Alex asks, nodding to my bookshelf where copies of my four Santa romance novels sit begging for attention.

"Uhh, well, I figured you knew already. Considering you snagged one at the shop today."

"Lea Steele, the author extraordinaire."

I nearly choke on my dinner. "Hardly, I write romance novels about Santa Claus."

Now it's Alex's turn to choke on his dinner. "I'm sorry. What do you write?"

"What? A girl's got to pay the bills, and it sells. Plus, it's kind of fun to write," I say.

"But you don't believe in the whole Christmas thing."

"I never said I didn't believe in Christmas."

Alex perks up.

"I just don't see the point in decorating for just me. I don't want to haul a Christmas tree up four flights of stairs and back down when it's dead. I don't own decorations, so I'd have to invest in them. I don't have any family decorations, and those are the only ones I care about. Not some crap from Target. You know? Plus, it should be about more. And for me, right now, it's just not. So yeah, I write sexy Santa fiction, and it helps warm the cold winter nights."

A smile slowly grows on Alex's face. "You're kind of adorable when you're worked up."

"Bugger off," I say, tossing a noodle at him.

Alex catches it and slurps it up. "Are you working on anything else?"

"I mean, I think I've always got a couple of story ideas in my head. But I don't always have the time to write them. What I'd give for the shop to be doing a little better so I could spend more hours writing."

"What would your dream novel be?" Alex gets up and helps himself to another fizzy water out of the fridge. "Want one?"

"Yes, please." I like how comfortable he is. "I think the dream would be a fantasy series. Something young adult where kids want to dress up as the characters in the book. I want them to be as excited to read as I was."

"The erotica Santa tamer wants to write for kids?"

"It's the dream. My last name isn't actually Steele. The publisher thought Steele would sell more books," I say. "Just a pen name. I'm saving my real name for the fantasy books."

"Uh, what's your real name?"

"What's yours?"

"Nickolas Alexander Snowcloud Claus the Fourteenth."

"The fourteenth?"

"Nickolas is a family name." His cheeks turn pink.

He's probably just glad I didn't mention that his middle name is Snowcloud. He probably has hippy parents. Not that mine are much better.

"Lea Lake Lovegood, the one and only."

Alex rolls my name around his tongue. "Lea Lake Lovegood. It suits you. It's a writerly name."

"The one thing my parents did right."

"Can't be the only thing," Alex looks at me in a way that warms me from the inside.

"Tell me about your family. Do you have any siblings?" I say to shift the subject.

"Only child syndrome here."

"Samesies." We high-five and burst into laughter.

"For real, though, I know what it's like to spend a lot of time alone, and I can empathize."

"But I thought your family was wonderful and cozy. Picturesque even," I say.

Alex reaches for his drink, buying time, no doubt. "They really care about the world in an epic kind of way. I wouldn't change that. But it also meant that I spent a lot of time wandering the property, making friends with—the help." Alex takes a swig.

"The help? Phew," I say exaggeratedly, "must be rough."

"It's not like that," Alex says. "It's hard to explain."

I shake my head. "You don't owe me anything. It's okay."

"I feel like I do," Alex sighs. "My folks run a charity of sorts. It always comes first. Always. I love it, and I've spent my whole life around it. But sometimes, I wish that I came first. It's dumb. I'm a grown-ass man."

"No, I get it," I say. "When my mom was alive, she put me first, and when she died, it was like I disappeared into the background."

"I'm so sorry."

I shrug. "It's not a thing I like to talk about. My dad remarried, and it was like I no longer mattered. I've lived an hour away for the last ten years, and he's never once come to see me. He doesn't call or try in any capacity. As far as I'm concerned, I don't have parents anymore. It's just me." I spread my arms, "And this town."

"Can I hug you?" Alex asks.

"I think I'd like that." He slides closer to me on the couch and wraps his arms around me.

Alex just holds me. He smells of cinnamon and pine. As if the man is made of Christmas cheer. I inhale him before letting him go.

"Looks like the sun is coming up," I say.

"I should probably go. Let you get a little sleep before you have to go open that wonderful little bookstore," Alex says with a wink.

A yawn overtakes me, sleep hitting for the first time all night. "I guess so."

"Can I see you again tomorrow night? Dinner?" Alex asks.

I hate to admit how much I brighten.

Damn boy.

"Tomorrow or today?" I ask clarifying.

"Umm, later tonight," Alex smiles.

"Good, that makes it sound sooner," I say.

Alex brushes a strand of my hair out of my face. "I've had a wonderful evening, Lea."

"Me too, Alex."

"Is it too forward if I kiss you?" he asks.

Heat blossoms in my body. I nod, unable to get the words out.

Alex leans in and brushes my cheek with his thumb.

I take a step, and my back hits the wall.

Alex takes a step forward, closing the gap, "You are the most enchanting woman, Lea Lake Lovegood," his voice is a deep, hot rumble. He brings my chin up to meet his mouth.

I'm caressed by a shiver running head to toe. His lips move on mine. Soft at first, and then the kiss grows deeper.

His body pins mine against the wall, holding me in

place. Somehow, he is teasing all the places he doesn't touch. All the places aching for his seduction.

Alex slowly pulls back. He leans to my neck and smells me.

He smells me!

"I look forward to dinner, Lea."

And just like that, he's gone.

I can't move. I'm pinned to the place he's left me.

What was that?

A shiver runs through me again. This time, I'm fully aware of the absence of him.

How am I supposed to go to sleep now?

I text Park, begging him to open the store for me. By a miracle of all miracles, he agrees. Sunrise yoga for the win. He'll demand details, but that's a problem for future me.

FOUR
Alex

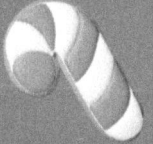

There should be an award for being in the presence of the most sexy, voluptuous, and intelligent woman and not taking her to bed when there was a clear green light.

I want to taste her slowly. I want to feel every inch of her slick, wet heat. I'm going to make Lea Lake Lovegood mine. I'm going to tease her until she begs me to come inside of her.

Lea would have let me stay. There was more than a moment. I've been with women. I've had women around the globe. But I've never just talked to one all night.

That sounds stupid.

But it's true.

I've never bared my soul to anyone.

This was never supposed to be more than a night away. Christmas is so close. My father will lose his mind when I tell him I'm not returning. The mental lecture is queued up in my head.

It was only supposed to be dinner. Maybe a hookup if she was into it, but then she opened her mouth, and I couldn't get enough of her.

We talked.

We just talked.

I need Lea in every way.

Back at my rental, I arrange more nights before calling my father.

"Does she know who you really are, son?"

"No, not yet. But I'm going to tell her," I say.

We hang up, and I realize he was far more supportive than I expected him to be.

Would she believe me?

Could a woman like Lea Lake Lovegood, without a single Christmas ornament in her home, believe in Santa? More than that, could she come to believe her Alex is Saint Nick?

Lea lost her belief in magic so long ago.

I'll have to find a way to show her magic is real. That magic can be utterly mind-blowing when used correctly.

FIVE

Lea

At two in the afternoon, I stumbled into the bookstore with a coffee the size of my head, which didn't look great on the boss. But then again, I am the boss, so fuck it.

"Girl, you walking straight today?" Park asks, rounding a corner with a stack of books in his hands.

"Rude." I take my purse to the upstairs office and lay my head on the desk.

"You were not out drinking all night. That hasn't happened since Natalie and Nhi's engagement party five years ago," Park raises a brow.

"No, no," I wave him away, grab my coffee, and head back downstairs. I turn and smile.

"You got some," Park slaps my shoulder excitedly.

"I did not," I say.

"The vat of caffeine would say otherwise."

"We kissed," I tease.

Park slaps my shoulder again. "Ooooo! Tell me, tell me, tell me."

So, I do. "Have you ever stayed up all night reading that book you'd been waiting months or even years to release,

21

and you can't help but think, I get to exist in the same world as you?"

"I mean, sure, but never a person," Park says.

"It was magic, Park. And that kiss," fire burns in my chest at the memory, slowly moving down my belly.

"Damn, that must have been some kiss," Park says. "You've just gone to a whole other place."

"You have no idea."

"But no sex?"

I slap Park on the shoulder. "I'm not a first-date kind of girl."

"Bullshit. You invited a stranger up to your apartment. I'm not judging. I'm just saying, own it." Park grabs a stack of books that need to be put out.

"I gave him a green light. I'd have slept with him," I admit.

"See, get it, girl," Park winks.

"But he's the one who left."

"Maybe he's the one who doesn't sleep with someone on the first night." Park shelves a book. "Maybe he wants a relationship."

"Ha! He's a Canadian tourist, Park. He's probably looking to get some and bail back to his maple leaves and syrup."

"If that was true, you'd have never spent the whole night talking. You wouldn't be floating on cloud nine, trying to talk yourself back down to earth," Park shelves the last book in his arms and spins to me. "When are you going to see him again?"

"Tonight."

"See, now go help that customer find the books on her daughter's wish list."

"I thought I was the boss," I say with a smile.

"Well, when you're messaging me at seven to swap

shifts, I think you give up the title for the day," Park says and walks off in the opposite direction of a customer.

I'm not going to check my phone five hundred times today. I have work to do.

My phone dings.

Alex: I can't wait to see you this evening.

Park walks by, "You can try to hide it, but I heard it already. Plus, your face is way too easy to read."

"He's excited about dinner tonight," I say.

"Awe, good. Now get back to work."

"Do you think Santa is real?" asks an eight-year-old girl holding a copy of *Where The Sidewalk Ends* and looking at me with big brown eyes full of wonder.

"Of course," I say, feeling a tinge of guilt at the lie.

"Alan says that Santa isn't real. That it's just your parents putting presents under the tree," she looks down at her book.

"Then it sounds like Alan's a real jerk."

Her head pops up, and she stifles a giggle.

"Why would Santa bring presents for Alan, some random kid who doesn't believe in him, when he could bring presents for a little girl who does? He's a very busy man, you know. He only visits believers, after all."

She brightens with a new outlook on Christmas. "Alan is a jerk." The little girl trots off to her mom.

"Well, that was a nice thing you just did there," comes a deep voice from behind me.

My insides liquefy.

I spin around and find Alex. "Hello to you, too."

"I didn't take you for a believer in Santa," Alex says.

23

I pick up the books I'd set down, suddenly nervous. "I was maybe a year older than her, and all I wanted was an art easel for Christmas. I'd written Santa a letter and made it to see him at the mall that year, too. My parents didn't have much money, but I figured Santa would come through. He was magic. On Christmas Eve, I went to ask my mom a question, and she was wrapping presents. I glanced at a tag, excited to see if it was for me or not, and it said from Santa. I was crushed. The next day, there was no easel, and that's when I stopped believing. When my mom died, I stopped celebrating."

I start to walk away, but Alex stops me. He pulls me in for a hug, and I let him. "I'm so sorry that happened to you. You didn't deserve that. Christmas should have always been magical."

I never expected to be comforted. I sigh and lean into him. He's warm and somehow still smells of— "Were you at the bakery this morning? You smell like sugar cookies and —" I nuzzle his neck and inhale, "a Christmas tree. How?"

Alex chuckles. "Thanks. I think there's a compliment in there somewhere."

"There was."

"What time do you close?" he asks.

"I just have to finish up with these customers and lock up. I can leave the rest for the morning," I say.

"Okay, I'm going to just," Alex points to a row of books.

I nod and go back to the counter to help the next customer.

Twenty minutes later, I grab my bag from upstairs and leave a bribe slash thank you as a gift for opening the store two days in a row for Park. I have zero intentions of letting this man out of my sight until tomorrow.

Maybe not even then.

"Are you ready," I say.

"You have such a unique little niche. I'm sure you hear it all the time," Alex says.

"Only from the tourists." I bump his shoulder, and he holds the door open for me.

"Well, it is."

"Thank you." I lock up and then find my courage. "I don't know if you had any plans, but I was going to suggest we grab a pizza and head back to mine? We could watch a movie or something?"

A smile plays on Alex's lips. "This sounds like a far better plan than anything I had in mind."

"Oh? What did you have planned?" I pry.

"Sure. You know, a restaurant, a movie. But with your plan, we can share a blanket and talk through the whole thing without being pummeled by popcorn," Alex grins wickedly.

"We basically have the same plan," I say.

"Great minds and all."

"The pizza place is around the corner," I try not to grin, but I fail.

"What's your favorite pizza?" Alex asks.

"Depends on the mood. I'm not huge on pizza sauce, so I'm a big fan of garlic cheese bread. Anything with pesto, sometimes you just want a super cheesy pizza, though, you know?" I say.

"Oh, I love me some garlic bread. And I'm big on the pesto. Whoever put it on a pizza," he kisses his fingers, "Chef's kiss."

We ordered a large pie and garlic cheese bread and asked for extra parmesan. I'm ninety percent sure I don't have any at home. I haven't had much time to get to the store lately.

We're waiting for our pizza, and it starts to snow.

Again.

"Couldn't have waited till we got home?" I ask the universe and cross my arms for warmth.

"You've got to be freezing." Alex takes off his jacket. "Here, Lea, please."

I shake my head no, "In case you haven't noticed, I'm a bit rounder than you. I'm proud of these curves, and I refuse to apologize for them. But there's no way your jacket will fit."

Alex steps closer until we're mere inches apart. His breath warm on my cheek. He places his jacket around me. "I'm all too aware of your curves, Lea. They are making me hard. You are a goddess. But you're also cold. Trust me? Put the jacket on."

I close my eyes partly from the heat of his words and partly from the inevitable embarrassment to follow.

Holding out an arm, Alex slips the jacket on one arm. I hold out the other, and he easily slips the jacket on the other arm. I find his eyes as he pulls the jacket closed around my hips and my breasts.

"How did you?" I can't even finish the thought.

"Are you warm enough?" Alex rubs my arms with his hands.

"Yeah, I'm better. Much warmer, thank you."

Alex smiles. "I think our pizza is done."

We grab dinner and take it back to my apartment. It's a silent walk back.

I've lost the ability to use words.

The jacket should not have fit me.

Look, I'm not going to get hung up on this.

It has to be incredibly flexible fabric. I feel it, but I think it's wool.

I glance at Alex, and at the same time, he peeks my way. I crack a smile, and his matching one dissipates the weird tension I'd built in my head.

Upstairs, I put on the goofiest Christmas movie I can find, which is how we land on *Elf*.

"God, this movie never fails to make me smile," Alex says, grabbing another slice of pizza.

"Do you want something to drink?" I say, standing and walking to the kitchen. I open the fridge and grab a fizzy water for myself. "Alex?" I shut the fridge, and on the other side is Alex.

"Do you have any chocolate syrup?" he asks.

"I knew I picked the wrong movie." I open the fridge and pull out a bottle of chocolate syrup. "Per your request, sir."

"He just made it look so good," Alex pops the top off the bottle.

I set my soda water down.

Alex moves closer to me. "But I was thinking it might be more fun to lick it off of you."

"Oh, gods above, I take back what I said earlier. I picked the right movie."

There's that wicked smile again.

Alex's eyes grow darker. He steps toward me, pours a little on his finger, and slowly lifts it to his lip, never breaking eye contact. He licks it off. "Just as I thought, it's missing something."

My breath catches.

This time, Alex grabs my finger and pours a little syrup onto it, then brings it to his mouth and puts my whole finger into his mouth. He slowly sucks it off.

"Much better."

I'm up against the counter, and Alex is kissing me. Slow at first and then deeper and faster. He explores my mouth and moves to my neck. Stopping briefly to suck on my ear.

My breath comes in short bursts.

"I have never wanted someone as much as I want you, Lea," Alex's voice is velvet.

I lift my arms, and he removes my top. I slip my hands under his shirt, feeling his stomach. I slide his shirt off, and he pours chocolate syrup on me.

I'm kind of surprised at first.

Then he starts to kiss and lick it up.

I'm lost to his mouth moving across my body.

He unclasps my bra, and I sigh with relief.

Alex starts to unbutton my pants and pauses. "Is this okay?"

Oh, my gods above, I'm somehow even more turned on. I nod enthusiastically, "Yes. Yes."

He slips my jeans off, and I'm naked. His lips haven't left my skin for more than the length of a breath.

Alex lifts me onto the counter and tickles the inside of my thigh. "You are the most ravishing woman, Lea."

"You're just saying that because I'm in a compromising position," I whisper in caught breaths.

Alex abruptly stops touching me.

I've never felt more naked in my life.

"Listen to me, Lea Lake Lovegood. You are a snack that I can't wait to taste. I'm going to make you come until you're begging me to come inside of you. Then I'll tell you every day what a goddess you are. Understood?"

I gulp.

Nod.

Take a breath and lick my lips. Thinking of all the ways I want him.

Alex caresses my thigh and kisses me. He cups my breast and rolls a thumb over my nipple.

I suck in a breath.

He moves to my neck again and slowly makes his way

down my body. First, my breasts, then my stomach, kissing each of my curves.

He spreads my legs apart, feeling my pleasure.

One finger explores my slit, his mouth on my thigh. Slow-burning kisses. He moves to my warm, wet heat. His tongue finds my clit.

I've lost my breath.

My words.

My ability to think.

Short, quick gasps.

He moves his tongue, spelling my name into infinity.

I can't breathe.

I grasp the counter. Spreading my legs wider for him.

I move a hand through his hair, wanting him closer. Wanting him to fill me with his hard, pulsing—

I reach for him but only grasp air.

He moves two fingers inside of me, rhythmically gliding them to the parts of me no man has ever found.

My head stretches to the sky, pressure building inside of me.

His mouth, on my clit, an arm wrapped around my thigh.

I grab the cupboard as the growing, pulsing moment of release comes to a head.

Out of breath, I feel absolutely spent.

No one has ever made me come by eating me out. I don't say this, but I'm feeling it.

I look at Alex with new respect and wonder. "Wow," is all I manage.

Alex licks his lips and sets the chocolate syrup on the counter. "Like I said, way better on you."

Somehow, his pants have remained on. A correction I can fix. With his help, I stand, then unbutton his pants so he is equally as naked as myself. I take in the view, in awe of his beauty.

The lines of his bareness making my knees weak.

Admittedly, it could also be the mind-blowing orgasm making them weak.

I grab Alex's hand and walk him to the bedroom.

"You ready to beg?"

I find his eyes and kiss him, tasting myself on him. Sweet and salty. He moves to my neck and then kisses down my back.

He lays me on the bed, and I rise to meet his urgent need, but he declines.

Only teasing me with his fingers instead.

"Are you begging me, baby?"

I can't find my words.

I ache all over for him. I'm lost in his touch. I spread my legs, and he's on top of me but not in me.

My god.

I wrap my legs around him, reaching for his shaft, but he wiggles away.

"Goddess of mine, what do you want?"

My breath is jagged. "I want you. I need you, Alex. Please? I want you."

Alex holds my eyes, "I need you to, baby."

He thrusts into my burning caress, filling me. Rocking inside of me over and over. He reaches a hand down to my clit and rhythmically runs his thumb over it in time with each plunge into my depths.

The pressure builds, "Come inside of me," I whisper as I claw at his back. My own blinding moment of release overtakes.

Two more thrusts and Alex fills me with his hot cum. He relaxes on top of me, kissing my neck. He slides to one side of me and plays with my breast gently.

"A goddess among humans," Alex kisses my cheek. He holds me tight. Wrapped in his arms, we both drift to sleep.

SIX

When I wake, I'm nestled into the neck of a stunning woman. Lea, I'm a lost man in your embrace.

I lay slow kisses on her, gently waking her up. Starting with the back of her neck. Tracing down her shoulder.

Lea stirs.

"Good morning, love. How are you feeling?" I ask.

She tenses momentarily and then relaxes into me. A flood of memories from the night before resurfacing.

"Mmmm," she moans, wiggling her butt closer to my unavoidable morning wood. "Is that your arm, or are you just happy to see me?"

"My whole being is happy to see you. From the first moment I laid eyes on you." I slide a hand over her stomach, and she spins around to face me.

"When you say shit like that, I want to believe you," Lea looks almost hurt.

"What's wrong? I—did I say something wrong? I meant every word," I say, my words tumbling out in a confused mess.

Lea takes a deep breath. "No. Just be honest with me,

okay? Don't play me. I'm here, and I know you won't be here forever, so don't pretend like you will. Let's just enjoy the time we have. Okay?"

I'm struck by her words. She thinks I want to leave her.

Lea Lake Lovegood, you have another thing coming if you think I'm going to walk away from you so easily.

"Nothing but honesty," I say.

"Yes," Lea smiles.

"Then I'll repeat it, so you believe me this time. My whole being is happy to see you, Lea. From the first moment I laid eyes on you," I put up a hand. "Only the truth."

She softens and bites her lower lip.

I kiss her.

Taking her into my arms, I trace light swirls over her body until she's physically shivering. Lightly, I brush my thumb over her nipple, and it immediately becomes erect.

Lea moans, the most beautiful noise I've ever heard. This woman's pleasure is music to my ears.

Slowly, I sink one finger into her hot, moist center.

Lea gasps.

I lift her on top of me and settle her slowly over my cock. Her entrance waiting for me to plunge into her sweetness.

"You are the sexiest woman I've ever known," I say, taking her in.

Her breasts are within reach. I take one into my mouth, licking, sucking, nibbling lightly. Just as my teeth graze her nipple, Lea guides me inside her.

Slow at first.

One hand is on my chest while the other plays with her clit, seeking her own pleasure.

With each pulsating need, I feel closer to this woman

than I've been to anyone before. I can feel her tightness around my cock growing stronger.

Lea finds my eyes, and we hold there as a frenzy of explosions rock her body. I come to my own fiery culmination, and we sink into one another.

I pull the covers over us so Lea doesn't get cold. She snuggles into my chest, running her fingers in circles on my side.

"Why did you come to Coral Cove?" Lea asks. "Right before the holidays? If you're close with your family and all."

I sigh, wondering when she'd start to ask these things. "There's a big push at work right now. This time every year. It can become stressful. I started taking a day away here or there when I could. Pick a spot on a map and go," I say. All of which is true.

Lea doesn't say anything, so I continue.

"I came to Coral Cove because many years ago, I was passing through with my father. Sometimes, he would take me on his work trips. There was a girl here who was working in a bookstore on Christmas Eve. She had red hair and was wearing the most beautiful frown I'd ever seen."

Lea lifts her chin and finds my eyes. Searching them for truth.

"She was upset about something. I'm not even sure what. But I could have spent eternity falling in love with that frown. As it turns out, her smile is even more captivating."

I let my words hang in the air. I hope, above all things, I haven't scared her away.

"Did you talk to this girl?" she asks.

I shake my head. "I was too chicken. She was a goddess, and I was—awkward. I still feel like that shy guy sometimes."

"So you came to Coral Cove to find some random girl you saw once upon a time, years ago, but with whom you never had a conversation?" Lea says skeptically.

"No. I came to Coral Cove because it was a place that held regret. I try hard to live a life without regrets. I came here to prove to myself there's nothing worth hiding from. She was just some girl who's probably moved on. There's no way she'd ever remember me. And I could put this little memory to bed once and for all." I kiss the top of Lea's forehead.

"Did you find her?" Lea asks, not looking at me.

"Yes."

Lea stiffens, and I realize she's misunderstood my story.

"Lea, you were that girl. I didn't know I'd see you again, I..." I trail off. "It was a moment, and to think I'd ever see you again was bonkers. But here you are. Still just as beautiful as the first moment I saw you."

"I don't know how you do that," she says.

"Do what?"

"Manage to make me feel like magic exists in this world."

I can feel an opening to tell her the whole truth, but I hesitate and it's gone. I hold Lea close to my chest until she has to get ready for work.

SEVEN
Lea

"Two days in a row, you traipse in here after noon like you own the place," Park says.

"Well, it's a good thing I do."

"Please tell me you've got a better story this time?" Park sets a book on a shelf and puts up a finger.

He helps a customer while I run upstairs, drop my stuff off in the office, and finish some paperwork. Just when I think he's forgotten, Park knocks on the door.

"Thought you could just hide out here all day?" he asks.

I finish making my notes and look up. "Nah. I've just left some stuff unfinished the last couple of days."

"I noticed," he says.

"I'm sure," I say, rolling my eyes. "I'm just about done. Do you need help downstairs?"

"We're two days till Christmas, so yes. I need you to get your elf ears on and your booty downstairs," Park says. "And when there's a lull, I expect to hear all about last night."

A woman of my word, the first lull we have, I spill and tell Park everything. "It's like I've spent my life thinking that sex was on a scale from one to ten, and let's be real here. I'm the only one who's ever gotten myself to a ten. A guy's gotten me to a six at best. Suddenly, I learned that the scale is really one to fifty, and now I can't walk straight. Two words: Multiple orgasms."

Park squeals, and I am all smiles. "Did he stay the night?"

I nod, "I woke up with his arms wrapped around me."

"So, it's not so far-fetched to think he's after more than a cuffing season fling after all?"

"I don't know what to think," I say, shaking my head and grabbing a stack of books to be reshelved. "He makes me believe in magic, and I don't think I can let myself. He will leave soon, and I will be left with a big empty bed again." I shelve another book and turn to Park. "Like I told Alex, we're just going to enjoy what it is while we're together."

"Bitch, you gave him an out?" Park says, exasperated.

"I'm avoiding disappointment, okay. Can't be disappointed if he was always going to leave. I'm just going to enjoy this for what it is."

"Mind-blowing sex with a guy who has a striking resemblance to Alexander Viking Dude?"

"Oh my god, right? I had the same thought. Darker hair and softer around the edges, but that same intensity."

"You deserve happiness, Lea. You also deserve to get that pussy pounded from time to time, so go get it, girl."

I slap Park on the arm, "RUDE!"

"Haha! You really got to loosen up, girl."

Park is saved by the chime of a parade of new customers walking in the door. The flow doesn't let up again until the end of the day.

By the time I notice that we've reached closing time, I'm

absolutely exhausted. "This might be one of the best sales days on record," I say.

Park smiles, "It better be. This place is trashed. You'd think small-town folks would be more polite. Yet here we are."

"Small price to pay," I say, closing out the register. "Will you lock up?"

"Sure thing, boss."

I grab the money pouch and start up the stairs when Park calls my name.

"Lea, you've got a visitor."

"Okay, I'll be right down." My stomach does a flip, hoping that it's Alex. I haven't had a moment to check my phone in hours. I drop the deposit into the safe, grab my purse and jacket, and walk back downstairs.

"Hello, beautiful," Alex stands at the door, arms behind his back. As I approach, he pulls out a bouquet of flowers.

Roses.

"They're beautiful," I say, taking them. "Thank you."

"Go," Park says. "I can finish here and lock up."

"Are you sure?" I ask. "I've left you a bit short the last few days."

"Go. But you're opening tomorrow. I'll be a little late getting in. I'll clean it before I go," Park winks, and I can't help but smile.

"Thank you, Park. Have a great night."

"You too."

When we stepped outside, I was surprised to find there was a sleigh being pulled by a horse.

"What is this?" I ask. "I mean, I can see what it is —"

"I wanted you to have a chance to live out a little of the fantasy from your novel. I knew a guy who knew a guy, and," Alex spreads his arms wide. "Come for a ride with me?"

This man really is magic, isn't he?

Alex helps me into the sleigh and then climbs in next to me. There's a warm blanket waiting for us.

"The only thing that could make this more perfect is if there was peppermint hot cocoa and it was snowing," I say.

Alex leans down and pulls out two steaming mugs. I look around, but I'm not sure where they were hidden.

"I come prepared," Alex says. "Misère, I think we're ready."

I take my mug, which is hands down the best cocoa I've ever had. It's way better than anything I've had in town.

We make it two blocks, and it starts to snow.

"Man, if this is date three, what should a gal expect on a fourth?" I say, snuggling up to him for warmth.

"Whatever you dream of, Lea," Alex slides his fingers between mine.

The horse has jingle bells, and they seem to play a rhythmic tune as we move through the streets of Coral Cove.

"The town looks so beautiful," I say. "I guess I haven't had much time to just stop and enjoy it, you know?"

"I understand that all too well. That's why I imple- mented these little trips. I wasn't enjoying the little things as much as I needed to. They helped a lot. Made me slow down and really take in the scenery," Alex sips his drink.

"Must be nice."

"Would you want to come back to my room this evening, Lea?"

My stomach drops. I wasn't expecting to go to his place. "Yes. That sounds nice."

We circle Main Street one more time, and then we're taken to a little place lit by red and green twinkling lights.

"Here we are," Alex says.

"This is cute," I say.

Alex chuckles, "I half expected you to tell me who owns the place, lives here, or once threw a kegger."

"Well, it was the Brightens, but I don't know if they still do. Obviously, it's a rental now, and I was never into the house party scene. But Park was, so he could tell you."

Now he's full-on belly laughing. "Perfect."

Alex unlocks the door, and I'm met with so much holiday cheer I'm not sure what to do with myself.

"Is it too much?" Alex asks hesitantly.

"No, no, it's—umm, a lot. But it's also kind of nice. Just a little different from mine," I say.

"That six-hundred-square-foot art piece called your home, without a single holiday ornament?"

"That's the one," I smile. "You going to make me dinner? I'm starving."

"I'm way ahead of you," Alex says. "If you could have one thing this evening, what would it be?"

"You."

His eyes darken, and a smile plays on his lips. "Madam, to eat."

"You."

He takes a breath and shakes his head. "If you want dinner before I ravish you, you're going to have to keep your comments to yourself. Or I will take you right here, right now."

Now I'm laughing, "Okay, okay, dinner first. Because I really am starving. There wasn't much time for lunch today."

"So on with it then."

"It's going to sound weird from the girl who doesn't have much in her fridge or the time to cook, but I've been craving chicken and dumplings. Something warm and homemade."

"We are so utterly in sync," Alex says.

"No possible way."

"Wanna take that bet?"

I shake my head. "There's no way you made chicken and dumplings for dinner."

Just then, there's a sharp ding as a kitchen timer goes off.

My eyes grow five sizes larger, and I follow Alex into the kitchen, where he pulls chicken and dumplings out of the oven.

"How could you have known?" I ask.

"Christmas magic," he says.

Alex dishes each of us a plate, and we take it into the living room, where there's a cozy couch we can eat from.

"I'm in awe of you," I say. "Thank you for this."

"It's my pleasure. I'd make you dinner every night if I could," Alex says.

We eat, and much like the hot cocoa earlier, this doesn't compare to anything I've had before. It's next-level delicious.

"I'm kind of surprised there's a tree, fake presents, and so many decorations in this place. It's so cozy and warm," I say.

"It's definitely one of a kind," Alex says.

I lean back, feeling cozy. There's a fire in the fireplace, and I'm unsure when it happened. But the crackle is music to my ears.

Alex lifts my legs onto his lap and slowly removes my shoes and socks. He massages my feet, and I relax deeper into the couch.

"Mmmm, that feels nice," I say.

Alex moves slowly up my legs until my tights provide no more give. He slips them off of me, equally as slow, admiring the length of my body.

I lay back on the couch, and Alex kisses my ankles. He

moves up the length of my legs. Slowly, he parts my thighs and gently bites the insides of my thighs.

My breathing has become shallow.

Alex slowly teases the folds of my inner lips. He spreads me open to the apex of my need. Tasting me, moving his tongue over my pearl of passion, and sending me to another plane of ecstasy.

I wiggle my hips, obeying an instinct I hadn't realized I possessed. "Alex, I need you."

He continues to please me with his mouth until I'm on the verge of coming.

"Alex, please. Please, please."

"Okay, baby."

For two point three seconds, I'm left cold and wanting while he strips and finds his way back to me.

I part my legs, and he plunges his thick hard cock into me. Thrusting deeper each time. I grab onto the side of the couch, holding on as the pressure and pleasure builds.

Alex reaches for my clit and rolls it between his fingers, sending me to climax.

For the first time in my life, I am not quiet. The whole world can feel my pleasure.

When I come down from the body high, I find that Alex is still hard. "Oh my."

"Oh yes," he smiles.

Alex helps me up, "How do you feel about sharing a shower with me, Lea?"

I nod enthusiastically, and Alex leads the way.

The bathroom is much larger than I anticipated, with a walk-in shower.

Hot water runs from three shower heads, so there isn't a bad place to stand.

"This is quite lovely now, isn't it," I say, stepping in.

Alex dims the lights and joins me. "I thought you might appreciate it."

His cock is still hard, and I can't help but reach for him. Alex's eyes darken. I hold him in my hands and wrap my fingers around his swollen member.

Alex kisses my neck until I can't see straight. I grab onto his shoulder for support with one arm, not letting go of his erection with my other.

He wraps two arms around me and takes my mouth with his. "May I take you from behind?"

"You can have me any way you like," I manage to say between ragged breaths.

Alex takes me by the waist and slowly spins me around. I grab onto the shower bar and bend to my ankles.

My ass is fully exposed to him.

He caresses my butt and draws light circles teasing me until he finds my slick heat and slides a finger inside. He brushes a finger against my clit, and I'm seeing stars.

I lean into him.

"Oh baby, you're so wet." Alex leans down and licks the length of my pussy. "I love the way you taste." He rubs my clit again and enters me with his iron-hard shaft.

I suck in air and obey his thrust, rising to meet a need deep within my core.

Alex moves his fingers over my clit, and lightning strikes over and over, coursing through me in electric waves. "Oh, Alex," I moan and come again.

He doesn't let up. Continuing to thrust inside of me, I start to feel the pleasure build inside of me again, only my legs are weak. "Alex, I can't stand."

He withdraws from me immediately and gently lays me on the shower floor. Kisses me deeply and enters me again.

Two thrusts, and I'm gone. Crashing against the waves of pleasure once more.

Letting go of any inhibitions, I moan into the night, releasing my pleasure.

Alex kisses my neck, and I realize he's still hard.

How?

"You okay?" he asks.

I nod.

He licks my nipple and sucks deeply. Suddenly, I'm ready to go again. I spin him over and climb on top. Impaling myself on his straining shaft.

My nipples ache with his touch.

I need more.

Insatiable.

"I think I love you." I don't realize the words have left my mouth before his release is met with my own. We come together. He fills me with his seed, and I'm so turned on I could almost go again.

Exhaustion wins out, though.

Alex cleans me up and tucks me into bed next to him. He doesn't bring up what I said.

I wonder briefly if he even heard me.

When he thinks I'm asleep, Alex kisses me on the forehead. "You are perfect to me, Lea Lake Lovegood."

I'm absolutely lost to this man.

He wraps an arm around me and falls asleep.

EIGHT

Alex

Lea is the most serene sleeper I've ever seen. And I should know. Not only have I been up all night watching her, too afraid I'll never get to see her again once she knows the truth, but I've seen a lot of folks sleeping over the years. Part of the gig.

When Lea stirs, I brush tendrils of her long red hair from her face.

"Mmm, good morning," she says. "How do you always smell like cookies and Christmas trees?"

"Christmas magic," I say.

She giggles and snuggles deeper into my chest.

"What time do you have to be at the bookshop?" I ask.

Lea stiffens. "I need to open. What time is it?"

"It's almost nine," I say.

"Ugh, I need to get up. I still need to go back to my place for a change of clothes," she says. "I can't exactly wear the same thing again." Lea sits up. "It's Christmas Eve. It's going to be busy with all the last-minute shoppers." She starts to climb out of bed, and I pull her back down. "Alex."

"I have something I need to tell you," I say.

"Can it wait until tonight?"

I can't find the words.

"I guess that's a no." Lea crosses her arms. "Is this the part where you tell me you're leaving? I knew it was going to happen eventually. I just." Her eyes start to water.

"Lea."

She quiets.

"You are the most amazing woman I've ever met. I've stayed in Coral Cove much longer than I should have because I couldn't bear the idea of leaving you."

I reach for Lea's hand, and reluctantly, she lets me take it.

She closes her eyes, ready for a blow.

"I've fallen for you, Lea Lake Lovegood. I have to leave, though," I say.

Lea pulls her hand back.

"It's okay. I didn't expect you to stay. I knew it would have to end eventually."

"Would you quit trying to break things off with me? I'm trying to tell you I'm falling in love with you," I say. I hold up a hand. "But there's more."

Lea sits back but doesn't say anything.

"I'm—well, you remember my name is Nikolas?"

Lea nods.

"Nickolas Alexander Snowcloud Clause the Four-teenth." I let my words hang in the air. Lea never put it together when I told her the first time.

She's shaking her head slowly. "I don't know what you're saying, Alex."

"I'm saying that my father is Nickolas Clause, the former Santa, and only by the grace of his love have I been able to spend extra time with you."

Lea's brow furrows.

"I'm Santa Clause, Lea. I have to go back and deliver presents to the world. But—"

Lea stands, "No. Why are you lying to me? Why can't you just let me down easy like the nice fucking guy I thought you were? Lea, it's been great, but I have to go home to Canada, not I'm Santa ho, ho, ho, this has all been some kind of fucking joke," her words are angry. Hot tears spill to her cheeks.

"Lea, I would never. I'm trying to be honest with you."

She's pulling clothes on, and I can't get dressed quickly enough.

"Lea! Please, just listen."

"Listen to what? Why couldn't you just let well enough be? Why did you have to spin this otherwise magical week into something absolutely messed up, Alex? If that's even your name," she wipes away the tears. "Oh god, I don't even know if that's your name."

"I never planned on meeting the woman of my dreams, Lea."

"Stop saying that," Lea's voice catches in a sob. "Don't stand there telling me all these wonderful things only then say you're Santa Clause. My god, you know how I feel about Christmas too. So, it's extra shitty."

"I'm telling the truth, Lea. I swear it. Just let me show you. Please," I say, running out the door, trying to follow her. She's already walking down the street.

"Don't follow me, Alex. I never want to see you again."

"Lea."

"Don't."

I watch her walk away until she's out of sight.

NINE

Lea

"Happy Christmas, Lea," Park says, holding a present in hand.

Tears fall, and I turn quickly, trying to hide them, grabbing a book to reshelve instead, but he's too quick.

"You're not really going to stand there and tell me you're okay? What happened?" Park asks.

A sob escapes, and I blow my nose into the tissues I've been carrying. "Alex thinks he is Santa."

Park stares at me blank-faced. "Well, is he?"

I tilt my head. "For real? You're not going to stand there and defend Santa to the courts. This is not Miracle on Thirteenth Street."

"Thirty-fourth Street," Park corrects.

"Whatever!" I toss a book across the room. "I let myself fall for him, and he lied to me. Instead of just letting me down easily, he lied. Not even a believable lie, Park."

Park wraps me in his arms and just holds me. "I don't know if you want to hear this right now, but maybe just enjoy it for what it was. You've been alone for too long, Lea. He brought Christmas magic into your life, regardless of who he really is. I haven't seen you this happy in a really long time."

I sigh, "I just wanted all of it to be real. I wanted him to be real."

"So he could be Santa?" Park says with a chuckle, and I smile for the first time all day. "People actually believe in astrology, so why is believing in Santa so far-fetched?"

I roll my eyes. "Okay, okay, let's get on with this day. I still have a vat of Chinese food to order before they close up, and then I have a novel to work on."

"Anything good?" Park asks.

"My publisher wants the draft of my newest novel by New Year's. I haven't touched it in days," I say.

"You'll get there. You're a badass, Lea. You got this. Santa or no Santa."

"Thanks, Park."

"Now, get back to work. It's Christmas Eve, after all," Park smiles.

I shove him playfully out the door. "Go be with your family. I got this."

"Merry Christmas, Lea."

After work, I drive by Alex's rental and am surprised to find it empty. Not just empty, but there are no lights. There is no tree in the window and no lights on the lawn.

Why would the owner have taken them down so quickly?

I push Alex out of my head, wondering why I'm doing this to myself. I grab Chinese food and head home.

"I wish I had a pint of mint chip and one last peppermint hot cocoa for tomorrow morning," I say to my empty apartment. But I'm not willing to go back out.

I set the takeout on the counter and let the tears come.

I've been such a fool.

I put Gilmore Girls on for the five-hundredth time, pulled out my laptop as if I'd actually write anything, and grabbed a fork.

Nothing sounds good.

I close my laptop, grab the blanket off the back of the couch, wrap it around myself, and lay down on the couch, letting it soak in the cries of my broken heart.

Eventually, I drift to sleep.

The sun peeks through the blinds and wakes me. At first, I'm a little disoriented, but then I remember falling asleep on the couch.

Only where am I?

I sit up quickly, my heart pounding.

There's a Christmas tree in the middle of my tiny living room. It's lit and covered with ornaments. There are even presents underneath. I look around the room and find a wreath hanging on the door and holiday decorations carefully and thoughtfully placed throughout my apartment.

"Hello?" I say.

No response.

My laptop is missing.

The food from last night is also missing.

I've absolutely lost my mind.

Did I hit my head? I pinch myself. "Ouch!" Nope, I'm definitely awake.

I stand and cautiously make my way through my apartment. My laptop is plugged into the charger. The takeout I purchased is in the fridge, along with some foods I didn't buy. There's mint chip ice cream in the freezer and a steaming peppermint hot cocoa on the counter.

I think maybe I was wrong.

There's a knock at the door.

My heart leaps out of my chest. I set the cocoa down and shuffle to the door. Hand trembling.

"Who is it?" I ask.

"Lea? It's me."

Instant tears fall, and I open the door slowly. "Alex?"

"I tried to tell you. I'm so sorry, baby," Alex says. "I never wanted to hurt you."

"You're really Santa Clause?" I ask, still processing everything. "Or a really good stalker."

"I'm really Santa. Although I prefer Alex, between you and me," he says.

I open the door wider and let him in. "How did you do all of this?"

"Christmas magic, baby," Alex says, brushing my hair out of my face. "You are the best thing that's ever happened to me. I never wanted to hurt you like that."

I sniffle, "It's beautiful." I pull Alex close, and he wraps me in his arms. "I love you, Alex Clause. I believe you."

Relief washes over Alex's face, and he kisses me. "I love you too, Lea Lake Lovegood. If you'll have me, there will be presents every Christmas, dinner every night, and me whenever you'll have me."

Warmth rushes through my body. "For always?"

"For always."

Sign up for Jax Wilder's newsletter and receive a collection of unpublished Coral Cove short stories. Meet familiar characters and dive deeper into the love and romance that Coral Cove is known for. Don't miss out on this exclusive content!

If you enjoyed, Sleighed by Love
Check out the next book in the Coral Cove series:

Harvesting Love

Ben:

It's the anniversary of my fiancé's death, and a weekend in Coral Cove was meant to honor the trip we never got to take. So, is it wrong that I'm falling into bed with the cute bookstore clerk? The chemistry is undeniable. But am I ready to embrace the magic Coral Cove has to offer?

Park:

Being best friends with the boss has its perks, like a discount on the latest spicy MM romance and the ability to knock off a bit early when a smokin' hot bibliophile pops into the shop. Thanksgiving is more about family anxiety than holiday cheer, until a chance encounter with good taste changes everything. Can I convince him to spend a little more time together, even if it's with my crazy family?

Step into Coral Cove, where the magic of Thanksgiving brings love and passion to life in this heartwarming and tantalizing MM romance. A man scarred by loss, looking for a fresh start in Coral Cove. His chance meeting with Park in the quaint bookstore sparks more than just friendly conversation. When Park and Ben's paths cross, the chemistry is instant and undeniable. What begins as an innocent meeting soon turns into a night of passion.

Additional Titles

3 of Swords
5 of Cups

Lorelai Hamilton
Find Your Bliss
Teenage Witch's Grimoire
Tarot Reflection Journal
Tarot Refection Journal Coloring The Tarot
The Eclectic Witch's Grimoire
Dream Journal
Teenage Tarot
Tarot Tales and Magic Spells
Arcane In Verse

Jax Wilder

Miranda Levi
From A Youth A Fountain Did Flow
The Sea Withdrew
A Tear In Time
Mo(ther) Na(ture)
In Orion's Hands

ADDITIONAL TITLES

Jackson Anhalt
From The 911 Files

Lorelai Hamilton
Find Your Bliss
Teenage Witch's Grimoire
Tarot Reflection Journal
Tarot Refection Journal Coloring The Tarot
The Eclectic Witch's Grimoire
Dream Journal
Teenage Tarot
Tarot Tales and Magic Spells
Arcane In Verse

Isla Watts
A Fairy Bad Day
Surprise! You're a Vampire
Gorgeous, Gorgeous, Gorgons
Mork The Handsome Orc
Adopted By Werewolves
Bite Me If You Can
That's The Spirit!

Rose Dawson's Book Journals
My Time With The Fairies
Enchanted Escapades
Enchanted Escapades
Dewey Decimal Diaries
Siren's Songbook

ADDITIONAL TITLES

Pride and Prejudice
Bibliophile's Bounty
Book of Books Journal
Pages & Passages Reading Journal
Bookworm's Companion Reading Journal & Tracker

Acknowledgments

Lea and Alex's story came to me in an afternoon, and I couldn't let it go. I was working on other things, and I just kept circling back to it, wanting to tell their little adventure.

Thank you, JJ, who helped me realize I had this kind of story inside of me. What started as a tease really came full circle.

And a special thank you to my husband. You are always the inspiration, baby. I love you.

Thank you to my readers. You are the reason I do this.

Jax Wilder

About the Author

Jax Wilder is a passionate romance author hailing from a charming small town nestled in the picturesque Pacific Northwest. With a heart full of love and an unyielding belief in the power of happily ever after's, Jax weaves enchanting tales of love and connection that leave readers captivated.

Jax's novels are a reflection of her commitment to celebrating the magic of love, and her characters' journeys mirror the warmth and happiness she has found in her own life. Join her on the enchanting journey of love, passion, and enduring connection through her heartfelt romance novels.

Jax Wilder

amazon.com/stores/Jax-Wilder/author/B0CM36CSH1?ref=ap_r-dr&isDramIntegrated=true&shoppingPortalEnabled=true